To Sonya + Bowen
Love,
Reg

belated or early 2006
christmas.......

A LEGEND OF SANTA
And His Brother Fred

With Very Best Wishes
Donald G. Henkel
2006

By Donald G. Henkel
Illustrated by D.B. Henkel

Quillpen

To my mother and father whose example of family and faith has drawn the map for my journey through life and to Jan who stands beside me with love.   *D.G.H.*

With thanks to Li'l "C" and with hope to all the children and handicapped of the world.

D.B.H.

First Edition 2000

Published by Quillpen
1520 Waverly Drive
Trenton, Michigan 48183
U.S.A.
Illustrations were done in watercolor and ink on rag board
The body text is set in 22 point New Century Schoolbook
Printed and bound in Canada by Friesens

1 3 5 7 9 10 8 6 4 2

ISBN 0-9673504-0-9
Library of Congress Catalog Card Number 99-97836

Santa's more to Christmas than mistletoe or snow,
Yet there are things about this man I feel you may not know.
Brave Albert was his father, Sweet Anna his dear mother,
And stories we've heard in the past don't tell about his brother.

And so...

D.S.H.

I'll tell you this short story
just as it was told to me.

It's a fascinating story
of how Santa came to be.

I think the story's factual;
I do hope it is true.

It starts when he was very young,
a child just like you.

He had a mom and daddy
and a little brother Fred.

Their parents hugged and kissed them
when they tucked them into bed.

As these young men were growing,
God showed them what was good;

So Santa and his brother
did the very best they could.

The family moved up north one year
where there was lots of snow.

They had to ride a reindeer
most every place they'd go.

They felt that they were stranded;
they didn't know what to do.

Then all at once their reindeer
jumped in the air and flew.

The boys were quite astonished,
but they took it all in stride.

It was the first time ever
for a flying reindeer ride.

It wasn't long thereafter
they found more could fly that way.

They put them all together
and hooked them to a sleigh.

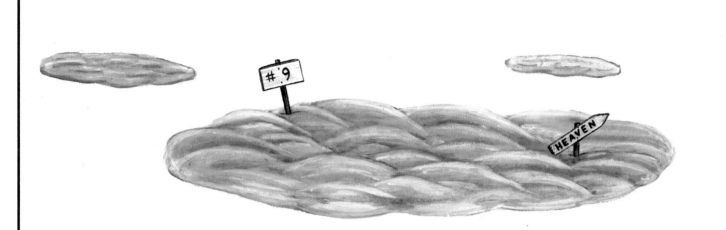

Now they had a team of deer
that numbered more than seven.

Fred and Santa took the sleigh
and flew clear up to heaven.

Now while they were up there,
God heard and saw the boys.

He came out to greet them
and filled their sleigh with toys.

He said, "I have a job for you;
'twill soon be Christmas Day.

Please take these to good boys and girls;
they're right along your way."

And so this was the first time
that Santa did his task;

Then every year thereafter
God did not have to ask.

Santa had decided
this would be his job forever,

So he delivers toys each year
no matter what the weather.

Now, I suppose you wonder;
where is Santa's brother Fred?

You never see him riding
with Santa in his sled.

Well, Santa and his brother
thought God had done enough.

They then built "Their Own Workshop"
To make all of their stuff.

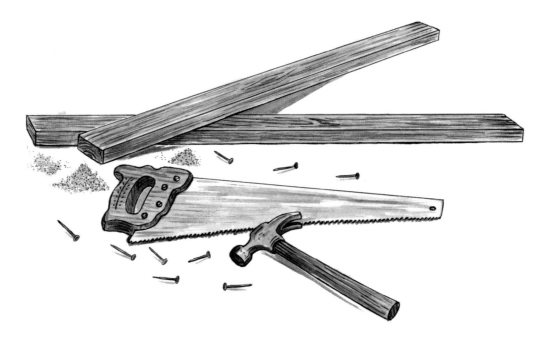

Then Fred became the leader
of ninety-seven elves,

And right there in their workshop
they make the toys themselves.

When Fred is not too busy,
he might visit in your town;

So if you ever see him,
be glad that he's around.

Now, does Fred look like Santa?
Well, I'd say just a tad;

But he wears a green, white-tasseled hat,
and looks more like your dad.

Now that you know this story
of these men in green and red,

When you write or talk to Santa
don't forget to mention Fred.

MERRY CHRISTMAS!

A Word About
The F and S Team

The Author

Donald G. Henkel was born in Middlebranch, Ohio, and spent most of his young adult years in Greentown, Ohio (Stark Co.).   He has resided in Trenton, Michigan for the past 38 years and summers on Northern Michigan's Cheboygan River. He has 3 children and several grand-children.   This is his first children's book.   A few of his other well accepted works include: "Down Home," "Christmas 1935," "Sentimental Treasures," "The Violets are Blooming," and "Take Time."

The Illustrator

D.B. Henkel was born in Canton, Ohio.
Studying art at the University of Wyoming and Arizona State further developed his fine natural talent. This is his first children's book. He is well versed in all phases of art, but his greatest pleasure is in sculpting. His unique sculp-tures won the "Artist's Award" in a recent nationally recog-nized art show.